MW01525934

Patryk Halkiewicz

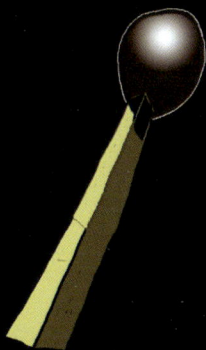

Stories
from
Around

Copyright © 2022 Patryk Halkiewicz

All rights reserved

Falenica - Toronto 2017/2022

ISBN: 978-1-915662-29-3

Drawings: by the Author.

Stories fine tuned: by Thomas Elliott.

Contents:

For my Grandmother (Babunia) and dog
Sambo, my best friends without whom
I won't be.

Acknowledgements

To say I am grateful.
To Thomas Elliott for his wisdom and
expertise in making the text readable.
To Ksenia Dobrzynska and Patrick
Halkiewicz for keeping up with
my moods and frustrations:
"no questions asked."
To Maria Etienne, who knew I wouldn't go
to waste.
To Jan Biluchowski, who is in our
dimension no longer - the man of
infinite patience, my mentor, librarian,
and the submarine captain - when it was
time to search the horizon with the
periscope made of old rain gutter
downspouts and elbows.

About the Author.

Patryk Halkiewicz graduated from the
Academy of Fine Arts in Warsaw, Poland.
Over the years, he worked on interior
design and furniture projects
internationally.
This is his first book.
He's carried its concept for a long time
but was too busy to sit down and do it.

The Green Parasite

Once upon a time, in the mid-fifties,
on a hot August afternoon a boy, whose
epidermal attributes differed confusingly from
those accepted in his native country,
was visited by his Mama.
Not the first visit, mind you, but
unexpected nevertheless.
Because the boy was confused, he found
a way to expect the expected not to happen.
This early developed philosophy matured him
significantly and he became a 500 years old
cynical S.O.B. at the age of six.
He listened secretly to the passing
suburban trains, to the sound of the
brakes at the station, to the minutes of
silence and finally to the sounds of the
choo-choo pulling away.

Being patient, he realized that his still young
Mama's high heels on the concrete sidewalk
wouldn't be heard for the at least next ten minutes.
The wait and the excitement was cruel
on his bladder.
Determined not to leave the look-out, he
delicately peed into his red woollen underwear he
only wore and felt an almost scalding stream
traveling down his thigh, knee and gently down,
until it hit the tip of his sandal, breaking into a
misty rainbow.
Tick, tick, tick – very thin steel heels on Mama's
shapely feet played a mysterious melody he often
sang in his dreams.
Expecting... Night and day. Day and night.
This almost mechanical, filled with clockwork
precision music made his yet short
physical existence worthwhile.
You pissed your pants," hissed Mama
"and you are filthy. Go and change!

He listened secretly to the passing
suburban trains...

I have to take you to town.
I'll be showing you to my friends.
Take this," she added, handing him
a small paper bag.
He ran home to his Grandma who helped
him to un-filth himself.
Mama waited outside, calling him to hurry.
In the bag, he found a light green cotton suit.
Short pants and a long or short sleeved jacket.
No shoes, no tee-shirt.
He was ecstatic.
He dressed up quickly.
No underpants and no tee. In his still wet sandals
he ran towards Mama.
"You look like a green parasite," she laughed.
Mama enjoyed to see him crying...
Then she started to walk back to the train station
with the boy in tow.
' I know who I am,' he stubbornly thought,
and didn't cry...

"Take this,"
she added, handing him a small paper bag.

Oh, how much would he give for a moment of having his hand held even so lightly by his Mama.
He would give up even on his new, unexpected and slightly too small green suit.
Holding hands was forbidden.
Well, remembering how old he was, he followed tickticks in silence,
His Mama sculpted lower back right in front of his - by the local standards - alien, slanted and wrongly tinted eyes.
The trip to Town was uneventful.
Maybe he's got shit from Mama.
Or maybe not...

Mama was a maniacal perfectionist.
Obedience, table manners, order.
She respected some of it, but to the boy this was just a blatant hypocrisy.

Holding hands was forbidden.

Oh, whatever... He had no say anyway.
From the commuter train platform
it was - by the boy's size – a long walk to the
amusement park.

It had merry-go-rounds with defective,
strange-looking animals: giraffes with their necks
cut in half for transport and reassembled upside
down, tailless horses, deflated elephants – neither
Asian nor African.
Some waltzing Matildas with dead eyes and no
waltz in them. Down-scaled Ferris wheel: six to
ride for just one turn only.
And...
And the quintessential swings in the shape of a
rowboat combined with a merchant ship, all in
peeling green paint. The paint exactly the shade of
the invincible Soviet T-34 tank.

It had merry-go-rounds with defective, strange looking animals

The boy felt a mixture of anxiety and disappointment.

Disappointment, because when inside the tank-coloured swinging rowboat he couldn't see much of the outside around him. Especially the amusement park's lights.

While the boat he's been in was swinging, slightly trembling, and squeaking, the boy couldn't imagine himself in a cockpit of a starship, passing galaxies back and forth. To where he never has been before. And no one else could for that matter.

Anxiety, because he lost sight of Mama. He lost her audio too. However strong was the initial momentum generated by the push of the strong hand by an unknown to the boy, but familiar to Mama man named Samson, that the heavy steel hull boy was in decided to slow down.

The boy fell asleep.

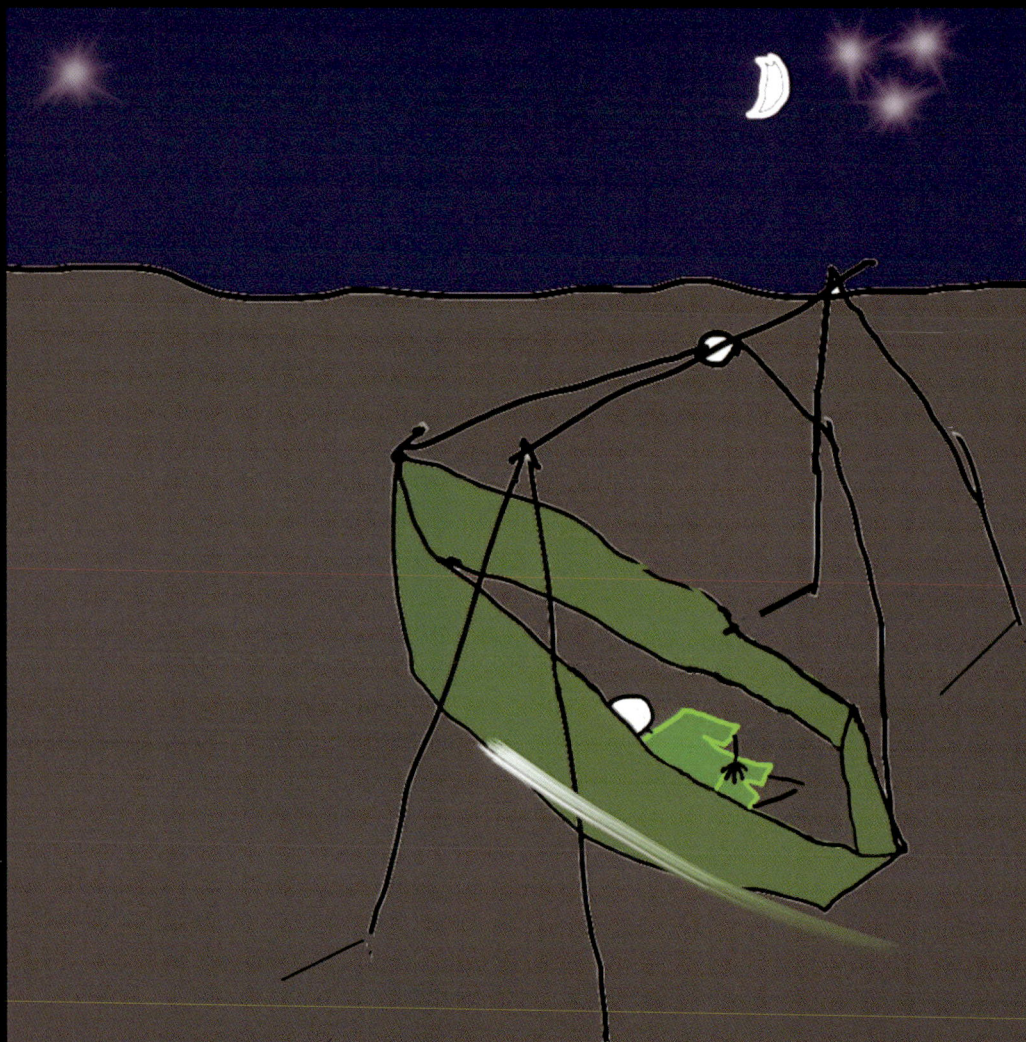

The boy fell asleep.

When he woke up, people were still milling around. The boat was moving, very slowly, high above the ground, from the boy's perspective.
His empty stomach came to life to the point of an immediate puke.

"Seasickness" - he figured. Too scared to jump off the moving tonne of a recycled T-34 and not to get hit or mangled by it, in a desperate need to vomit which,
being taught by his Mama, can not be done in public, the boy was seriously confused.
He was thinking hard, thinking hard.
He fought with his screaming stomach and with his upside-down digestive system, so he did not speak.
Then a big hand grabbed the collar of his suit and an equally big face of a fake Norma Jean appeared above him, curled on the ground below boat's keel bottom. He fought his screaming stomach and, with his epileptic intestines he did not speak.

samson!
samson!
samson!!

when he woke up, people were still milling around

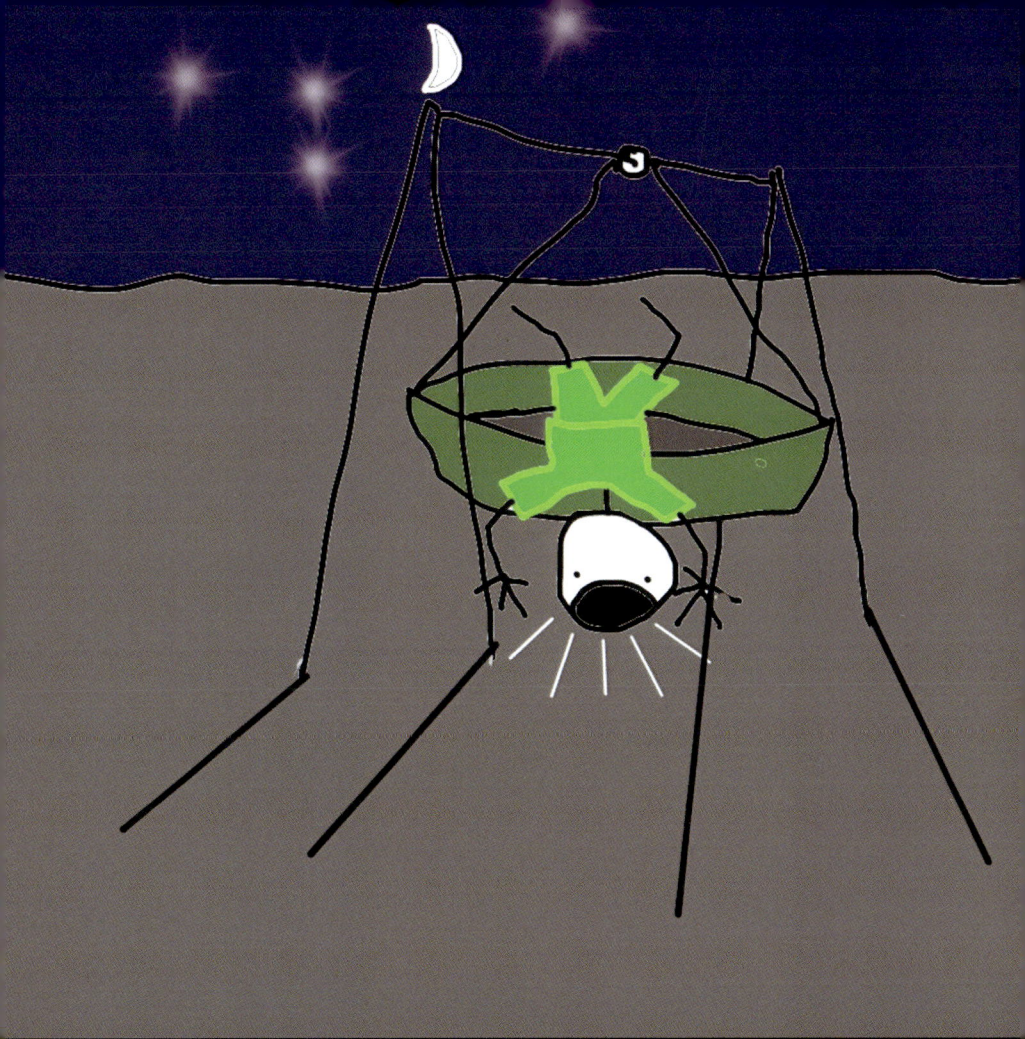

He fought with his screaming stomach...

"Come on" - said the big fake blonde,
extending her big hand.
The boy lost his balance on the boat's edge while
trying not to spray the neighbourhood with the
contents of his void belly.
He slipped from the big blonde's gripping hand,
fell on the grey and now black sand erupting
straight down a fountain of emptiness.
The Fake Blonde helped him up. "Where's yo' ma?
Where's yo' dad?", she asked.
The boy didn't know.
Cell phones were still a sci-fi and the walkie-talkie
was history.
'Samson" - the boy said
"Aha, this dump. It's a long walk.
So you go towards the Royal Palace, see up there?
You won't miss it, in a couple of hours you'll be
there,". "Nice suit," she said.
So he went. The persistence of his six years, exotic
looks in a suit opened hearts of the passersby.

...erupting straight down a fountain of emptiness.

"Where's yo' ma? Where's yo' dad?", she asked

The City nation didn't like foreign too much, but close to midnight, on the weekend meeting a lone, strange looking and fairly resolute boy:
"Oww fuck, look, he's all by himself, goes to find his mama, look, boy, yo' not too far, see this church, right next to it, on the corner, she's there every night. A regular. Not bad good looking chick. Nice boobs too. Your worked them, eh?
Sucking long and deep... Oww shut the fuck up, he's too small to get it... Yo fuck!
Boy, don't listen.
Go now.
Ask Lola at the bar. Brave fella. Fuck. Long fucking walk from down the river. Shit man... Middle of the night...".
The voices bouncing from the rebuilt ruins faded, came back and faded again. Vanished.
He walked. The night was hot and humid. He was green from hunger and from puking. Greened more by the reflection from his suit he walked.
To find his Mama.

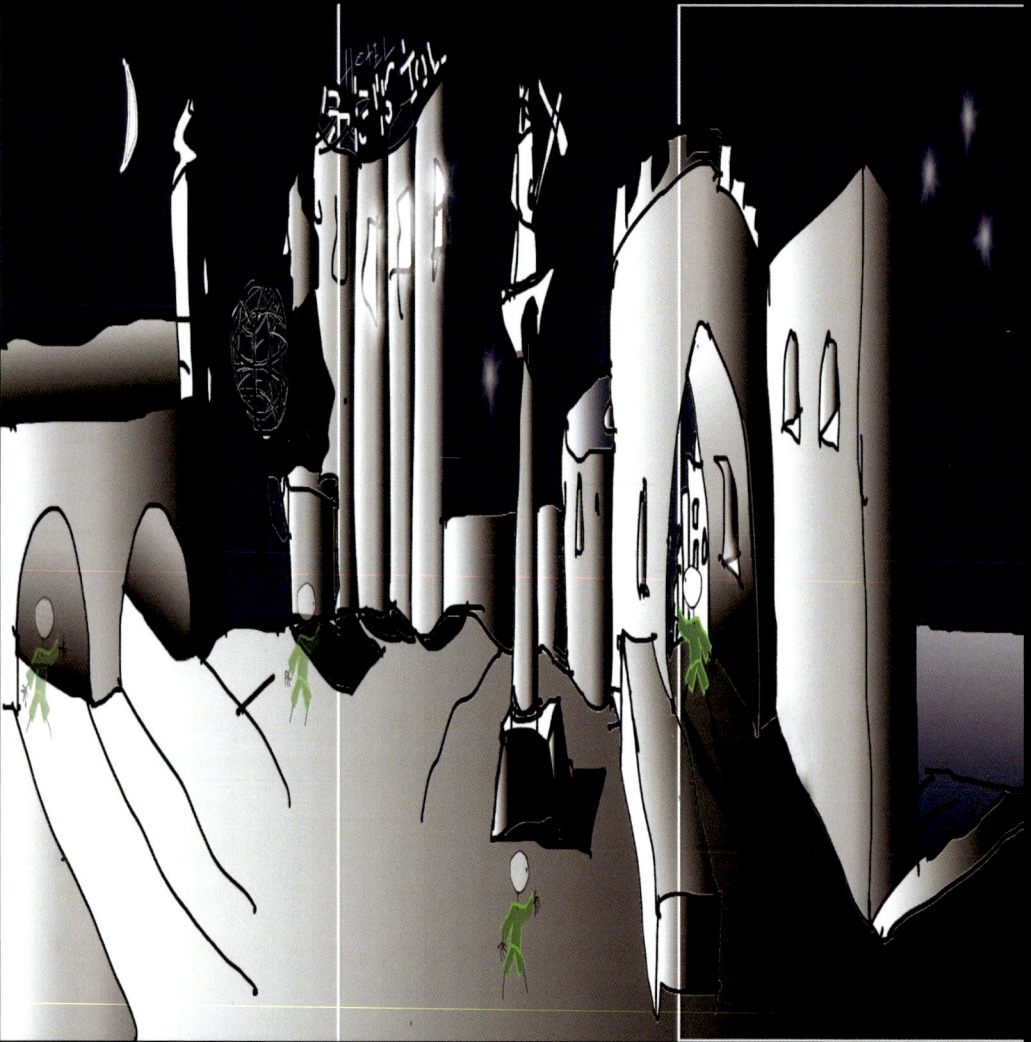

He walked. The night was hot, humid...

Paedophiles on the City streets were also a sci-fi in midfifties. But you could see and use or be used by them in certain, well-known institutions with which the boy was not familiar yet. Neither did he know what the Future has in store for him. Maybe some other time...

SAMSON!!!

Lights in the windows, smell of food oozed through glass and through the open doors.

Noise, screams, laughter, all underlined by the stench of legal and illegal booze, by the aroma of schnitzels and potatoes made his head spin.

The boy went in. The fake, fat Norma Jean - different than the one in the amusement park, but fat anyway dropped her big head to his original-and-unusual-eye-level and said "She's down there, to the left", then pushed him in that direction gently and yelled:

" Yo, bitch! Yo stray found ya!".

SAMSON!!!

The boy walked and stood close to the table with his Mama and a few happy men sitting around it. Tabletop, full of empty and not too empty bottles, ashtrayed food plates, half-eaten steak tartars and hard boiled eggs, crowned with cigarette butts made his stomach growl.
He asked it to stop. Successfully.
He stood. The table was quiet...
Nobody moved. Mama's jaw was down.
Almost to the ground.
Confusion, anger and disbelief burned in her watery, blue eyes.
The whole room jaw dropped. Aha!
To the ground.
The boy would say an "f " word.
But he did not swear. Yet... So he kept quiet.

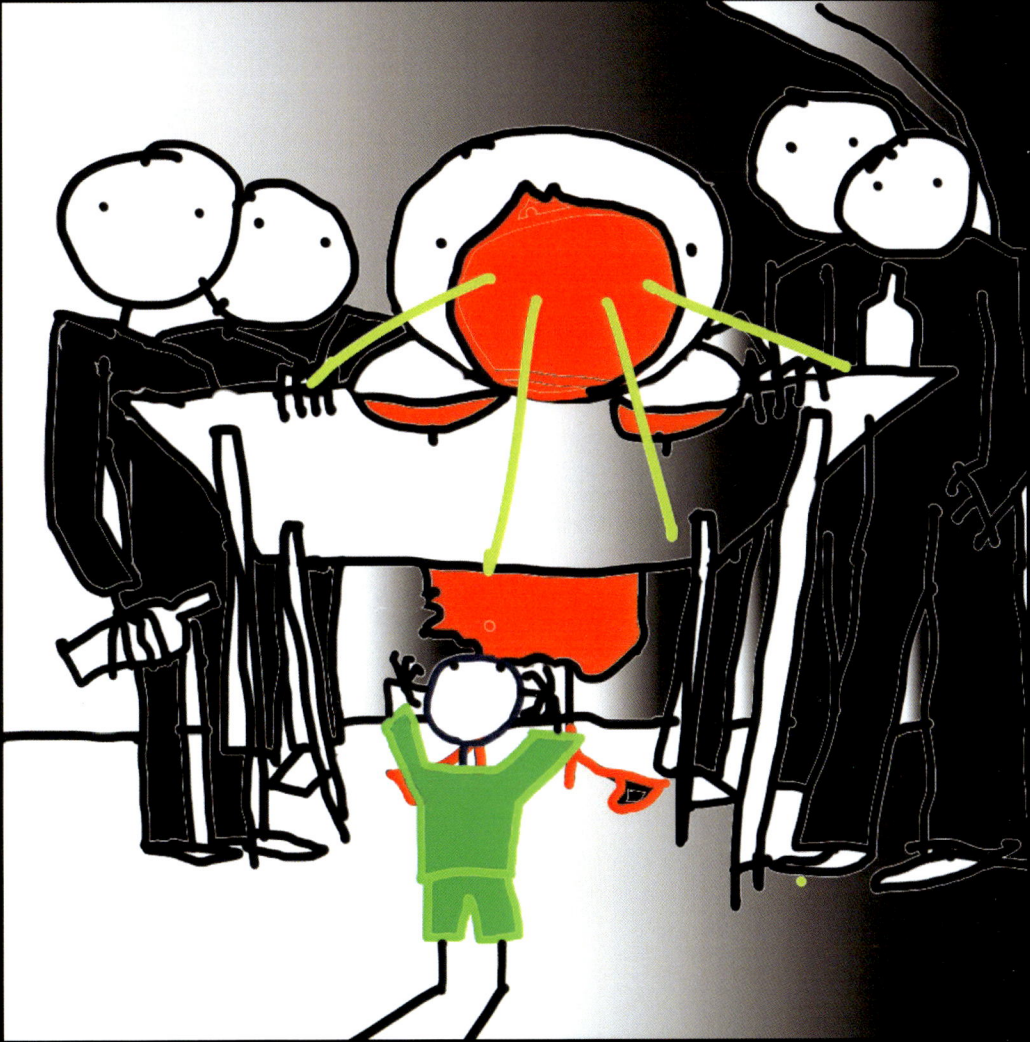

Then Mama erupted: "This is unbelievable!"

Then she erupted "This is unbelievable! I was really hoping he'll get lost, got kidnapped or drowned!!!".
The room exploded with drunk laughter. Mama and her company continued into their affairs.
Fake Marilyn Monroe squeezed a greyish but tasty piece of hard boiled egg into boy's mouth.
Whether it has been adorned previously by the cigarette butt, he didn't know and couldn't care less.
Cell phones were still a sci-fi...
Back in the suburbs boy's Grandma was going nuts...

The end.

(Ya think ?) .

The Swim

Once upon a time, when Fahrenheit and Celsius stopped to compete and were matching their numbers exactly, a boy, green-brown from summer exposure was digging a hole under the acacia tree.
"What's underneath?",
"You dig. You'll find out", his Grandma said.
Besides, to the tree the boy was more of a symbiotic creature than of any peril. Also, he liked to hug the roughness of the tree bark.
When doing this he almost disappeared within the textures and shadows and the tree was touching boy's arms and licked his hands.

On this hot Sunday the boy was waiting for something special today.
It was a swimming lesson promised and expected for a long time.

"You dig. You'll find out", his Grandma said.

...the boy was more of a symbiotic creature.

Delivered?

Not yet and, Summer was to be over soon.

He heard the clap, clap, clap. "Slippers..."

It was the sound of his Mama approaching.

"JOY!".

Mama yelled: "Let's go, let's go!", seemingly in a hurry for a reason to the boy unknown.

He hurried...

Tried to put his hand into Mama's...

And was rejected.

He's gotten used to it. To being rejected, that is.

But he was determined not to quit. Regardless.

No matter how fantastical was the chance to feel the Mama's fingers.

The touch made him feel that he belonged.

Even that glimpse was worth it.

Life was good.

The trip took awhile.

Mama walked and the boy, half-naked run behind, sweating without noticing.

He kept the urge to pee under control, afraid to interrupt the walk until the river shows up.

The smell of rotting mud enveloped both. Down the dune, a lazy river was flowing, bouncing the oily Sun away from its mass, while Mama collapsed on the remnants of an old sandcastle, which shrunk even more. The boy wanted to run into the dark water but wasn't sure he could.

In the meantime, Mama was inflating the air mattress.

Mesmerized, the boy watched its mangled carcass taking shape.

Mama was pissed off and out of breath.

Her attractive exterior prompted no one around to offer a helping blow. Or two.

Funny, but it was exactly what Mama had in mind.

"It is the useless me", thought the boy

Then, pulling the mattress behind, Mama walked into the river.
When knee-deep she called the boy to jump onto the floating shape and started to tread towards the middle of the current.
Deeper and deeper, until only her head was sticking above the surface.
The boy, gripping the mattress' seams tried to assess the vastness of his watery surroundings.
"Time to swim!", Mama urged.
The boy, pretending to be confused about what that meant was given no time to get it.
The mattress was flipped violently and, what was the top became instantly the bottom, with the boy glued to its upside-down surface.

...until only her head was sticking above the surface.

The mattress was flipped violently.

The light had changed. It was as oily as before, with brownish tint and with the sun divided into a number of circles... Some square, some wavy. Underwater his fingers lost their grip. The mattress let him loose and he became much lighter.

Looking around – eyes wide open – he swerved to avoid some leafy underwater plant and saw the murky side of a lazily traveling fish. This one was doomed to be dead soon.

For as he remembered the only fish alive would be a Christmas Eve carp at the local grocery store.

To get it, the boy would be meeting other boys and girls in the freezing, early morning hours in the fishy queue.

...the boy would be meeting other boys and girls...

He couldn't see the river floor nor its surface
at the moment.
Just the sun rays in an epileptic dance trailing the
fish's wake...
"So different, so cool..."- the boy was thinking.
He wanted to see, to explore more when suddenly
he realized that he needs air. Faithfully expecting
his Mama to be right beside him, thinking that she
knew for how long he could hold his breath.
Water replaced oxygen in his lungs.
He tried to exhale. Then to inhale. Still no air.
The liquid full of sand particles scratched his
trachea, entering the depths of his
pulmonary region.
His unconscious mind and water filled body
floated downstream, just slightly below the surface.

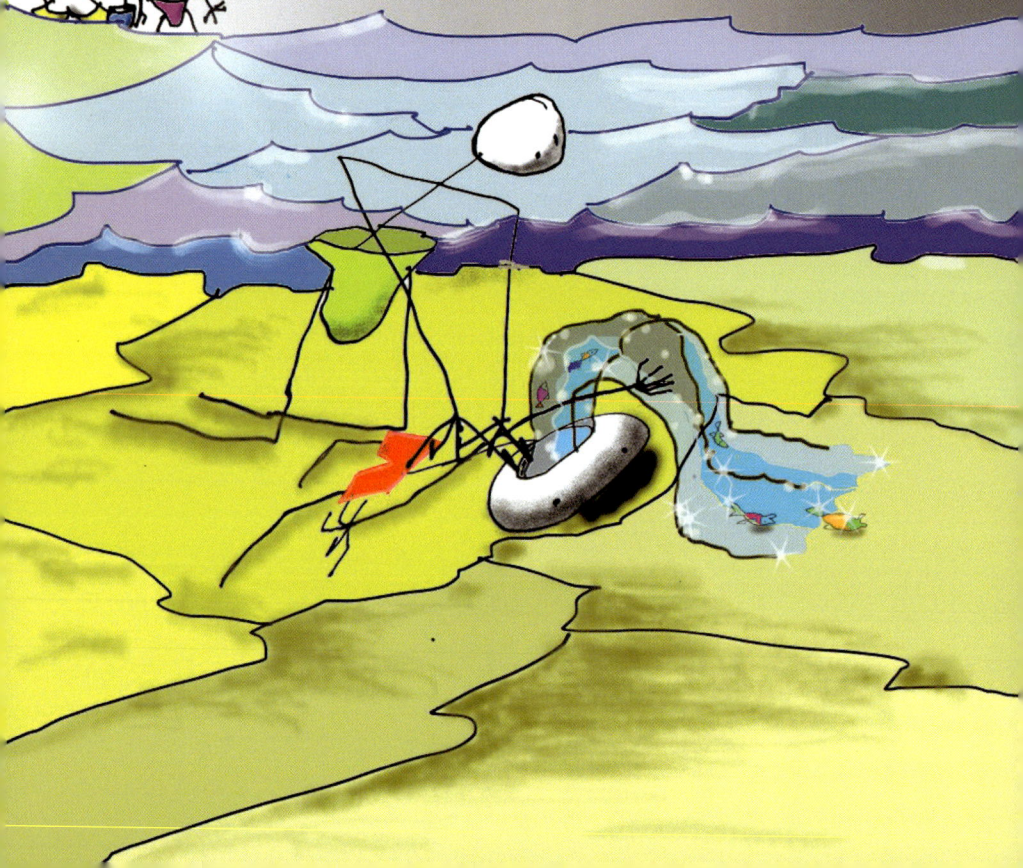

When he opened his eyes and spat hysterically
volumes of water from himself,
he was laying on a sandy beach with a man
pumping his chest fairly gently.
"If I wasn't there and didn't pull him out,
he'll float down to Sweden!.
"Cadavers don't get refugee status, didn't ya
know?!".
Angry and in complete disbelief
the man was yelling, obviously not satisfied with
Mama's explanations.
The boy sat up.
Disoriented as he was he saw the mattress.
A faraway little blue and red dot moved slowly
along with the current.

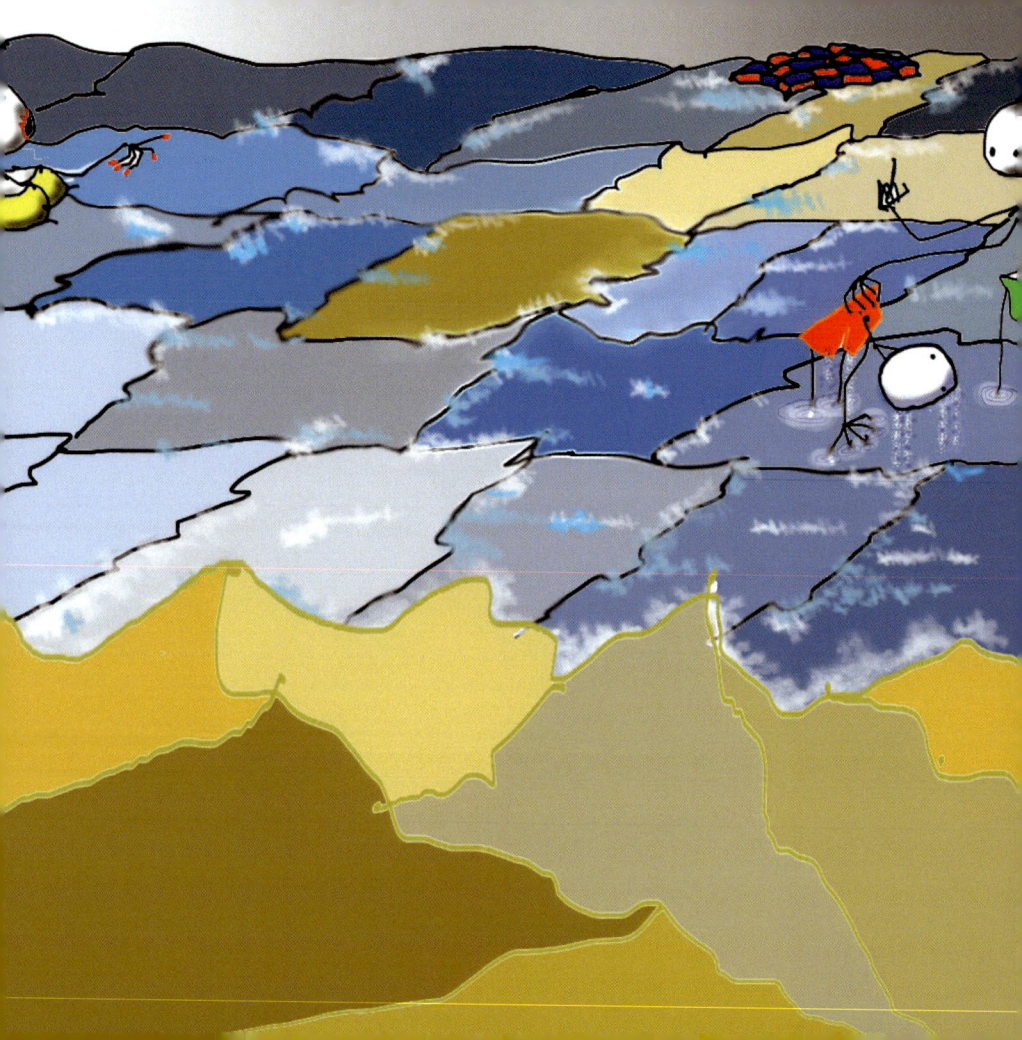

While the man walked away, the Host, shaking her head and muttering obscenities looked at the boy and said with the utter disgust "I knew it! I knew! You don't know how to swim and you never will! Above all you lost the mattress!", and walked away, picking up the towel along with the beach bag. Then she was gone and it was getting late. The boy knew the shortcut to get home and went to bed before Mama was back.
If she ever did.
Years later the boy won
a few swimming championships.
Not important enough to boast about it.
Was he on an inflatable mattress again?

He didn't say.

the boy won a few swimming championships

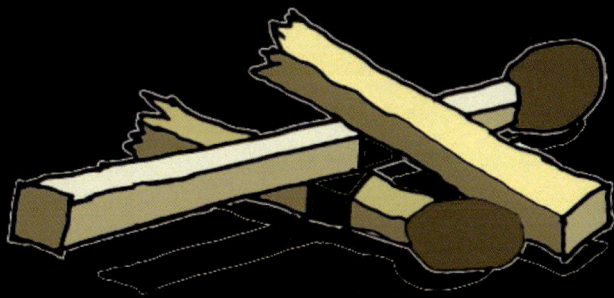

The Island

It was the fresh and salty smell of the air and the wavy noises only the waves can make.
"It has to be an island," they figured.
So... The island it was.
That's how they've named the place and, except for some slight external disturbances they sat mute and still.
After a while, their fear shape-shifted into curiosity.
They turned around to see each other and tried to figure out who the fuck they were.
The nightgowns they wore came from the different fashion labels.
"Does anyone have a smoke?" asked one of them.
"I do," said the other.
"Can I get one too?" pleaded the third.
"Sure, but that's it folks," said the first,
"It's just matches what I've got left."
It did not seem strange about how easy the conversation went.
Almost as they were on some social media network.

and the wavy noises only the waves can make

"Does anyone have a smoke?" asked one of them

The three of them sat back to back

The three of them sat back to back in a
flawed shape of the star of David,
enjoying the rich flavor of the plain Pall Malls.
The ritual was slow. Too slow maybe,
 effectively generating little burns at the fingertips.
"So, what's next?" someone said.
"Let's draw."
"OK. How?"
"Top half for the God, bottom half for the angel,
and the devil gets a full one."
The draw took place, and in an instant, after its
conclusion, all three found themselves
appropriately dressed for the roles drawn.
God chose a comfortable seat in a sandy niche
covered from the wind, just a little above the flat
rock platform for himself.
He sat cross-legged, resting his back against
the rock behind.
The rock was soft.

"So, what's next?" someone said.

The rock was soft.

The Angel glanced at the Devil. The Devil glanced back and the duel began.
The Devil fought with a Turkish saber, the Angel with an unusually long-stemmed white lily.
An interesting choice of weapons, but even so the stem proved to be as hard as the Damascus steel.
Both blades hummed to the tune of a murderous melody for a while.
Then, suddenly the Devil lowered his weapon.
"I quit," he said.
The Angel with his usual and unbearable honesty dropped the lily on the ground and looked at God for a sign.
God just shrugged.
In an instant, the Devil lunged forward and, with ferocious force, cut the Angel's head off, resulting in the Angel's violent convulsions and his subsequent collapse.
His head set off to be a high flying object disappearing into the sun's glare.

...and the duel began.

...a high flying object disappearing...

His body dropped on top of Angel's lifeless remnants...

In an instant, the Devil lunged forward and,with
ferocious force cut the Angel's head off, resulting
in Angel's violent convulsions and a subsequent
collapse.
His head set off to be a high flying object
disappearing into the sun's glare.
The Devil knelt to wipe his bloody saber
on the Angel's red soaked snow-white robe.
In the meantime, gravity took control
over the Angel's flying head, preparing it for
touch-down.
His saber sparkling, the Devil started to rise when
the falling head struck his own.
He died instantly. His body dropped on top of
Angel's lifeless remnants shaping a cross made by
his cadaver and the other's.
No convulsions occurred at this time.
The fog started to thicken.
God held his position until the visible becomes
invisible and the Earth returned
to its original flat shape.

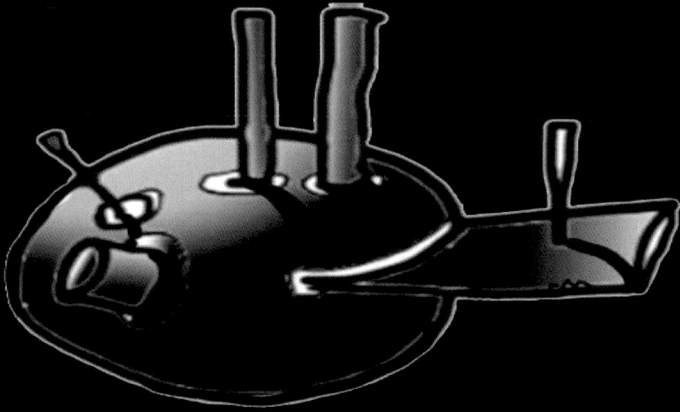

The Machine

...the owner of a machine.

One day a village found itself to be the owner
of a machine. There was no indication where it
came from. Six villagers couldn't move it not even
one inch. More people gathered around.
Pushed and pulled... To no avail.
Felt themselves offended.
Attack with stones, axes and scythes proved futile.
Local priest, dramatically and roughly exorcised,
baptized and condemned the monster.
Still, the machine sat immobile, silent and heavy.
A local kid, considered by everyone an idiot
was watching the struggle from far away.
Couldn't be any closer.
Otherwise, like it always happened before
he would get ridiculed, mauled and
thrown head first into the mound of the hot,
fresh manure.
Wise villagers knew that the smell will precede
him, so he'll be ambushed again and manured

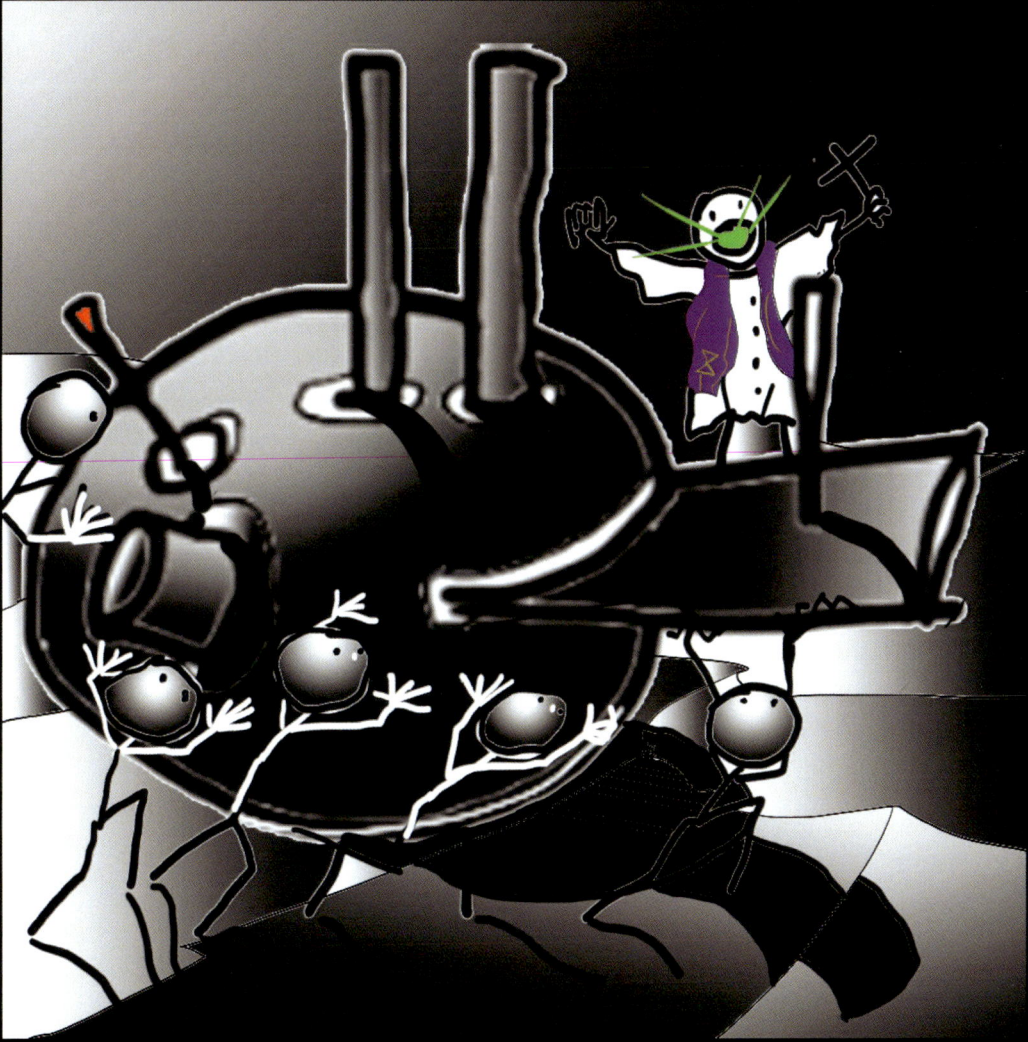

Local priest dramatically exorcised...,

Still, the machine sat immobile, silent and heavy,

Time to lunch. The sweaty crowd led by the angry, barely sober priest dying for a drink left the machine, heading towards small chapel for a quick prayer and then to grab a bite at their homes or in the pub. Lunch took longer than usual – so much to discuss. And that damn thing still out there, where it was left, on the hilltop.

Aww, screw it! Lets have another one...Tomorrow's on its way. If the thing stays where it stays, it'll be there for the next day too, they reasoned. And they had another.

The local idiot waited for the Sun to go down or for the Earth to move. When it happened he left his hiding spot and marched, this time unobserved towards the bulky outline blending with the hill's summit. Once there the kid looked up at the dark mass and beyond.

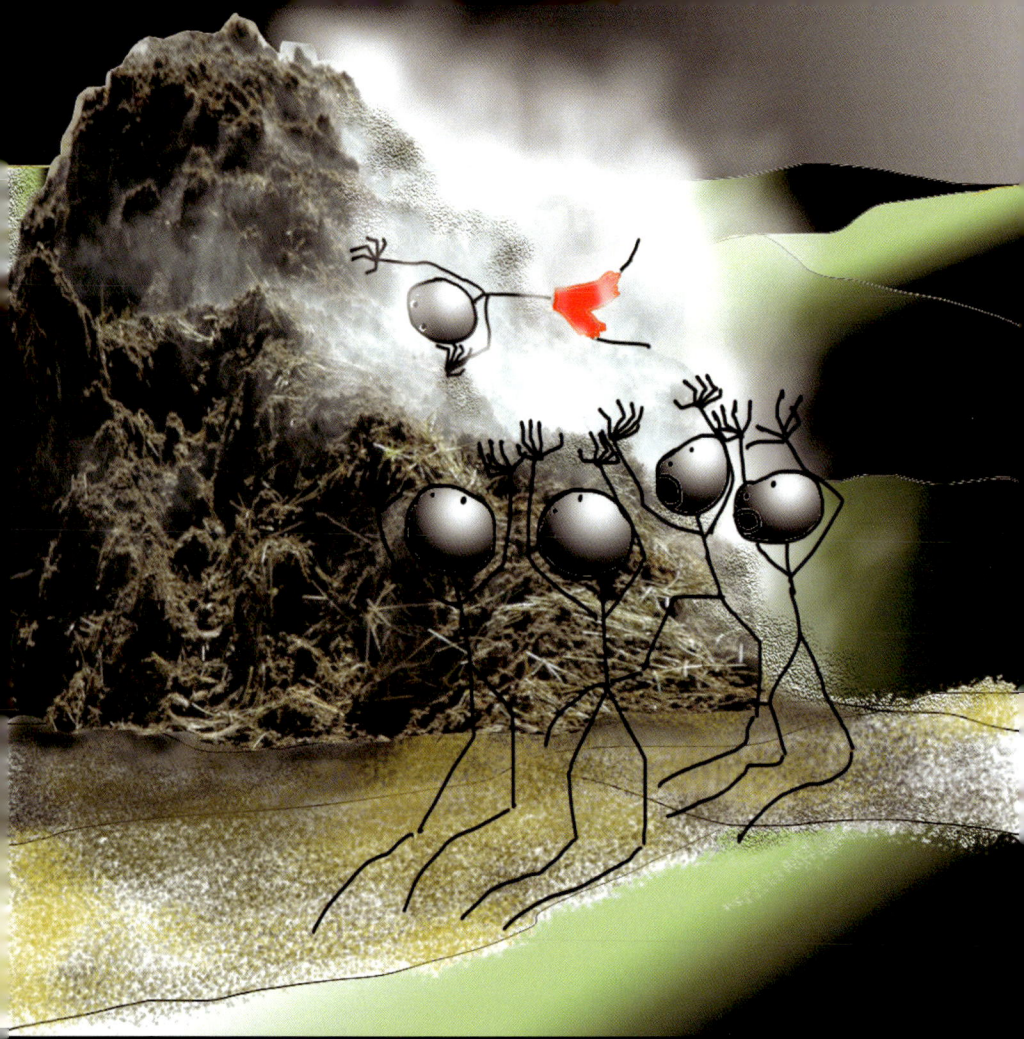

...he would get ridiculed, mauled and thrown

On the night sky silky fabric a bright and distant dot
rolled lazy and indifferent. A satellite perhaps,
thought the idiot. Whatever...
Finding footholds through different parts and shapes
he climbed the machine.
He sat for awhile, slightly short of breath.
Once rested, he started to explore surfaces,
protrusions, and collapses of the structure beneath
his feet, gently searching cold metal with his
manure-soiled hands.
On the night sky silky fabric a bright and distant dot
rolled lazy and indifferent.
A satellite erhaps, thought the idiot.
Whatever...
Finding footholds through different parts and shapes
he climbed the machine.
He sat for awhile, slightly short of breath. Once
rested, he started to explore surfaces, protrusions,
and collapses of the structure beneath his feet, gently
searching cold metal with his manure-soiled hands.

Lunch took longer than usual...

It was fairly smooth, not unpleasant and non responsive as well, but in the middle of its carapace a two-foot-long metal lever of unknown color - in the darkness it was irrelevant nonetheless – was sticking out. The kid, like every other kid, even for a local idiot-kid, was curious...

A lever is meant to be levered, no? So he pulled, pushed and nothing happened.

Then, as it was obvious to any kid, even to an idiot-kid, he moved the lever sideways.

Silently first, the machine rolled downhill and while gaining momentum it started to make a gentle rumbling noise, which could not be heard neither by the priest in his drunken state of communion with the Sublime Being nor by well past another one villagers in the local joint.

The chapel, the village and the pub were built on a common longitudinal axis. Maybe by accident - who knows - it was also the same for the fast rolling tonnes of metal...

In less than a minute all buildings ceased to exist, mowed
to the ground with all their contents.

...snuggled in and fell asleep instantly.

In less than a minute all buildings ceased to exist, mowed to the ground with all their contents.
The machine with the boy holding the lever stopped some fifty feet later, right in front of the manure pile. The local idiot-kid jumped off the mechanism and walked towards the mound.
Once there he dug a hole just wide and deep enough for him to fit, snuggled in and fell asleep instantly.
And the machine..?
Well...
Made a dig for itself * /stays as it was * /rusts in peace in a nearby fishpond *.
* - readers' choice.

The Flog

School day. Winter at her blast. Going across the track was fun. Playing cat and mouse with the incoming train. Practising nerves of steel. Just how indigenous hunters did. And leaving a stone on the track, seconds ahead of the locomotive's front steel wheels. The stone explodes, locomotive wobbles, just a little along with the engineer's teeth – if he had any in observation of primordial oral care in our Motherland. Sometimes the train was long enough for an excuse to be late in class. Also, snow played a crucial role, specifically for the boy, whose feet grew and were overflowing the last year's shoes.

Grandma accommodated the growth. She just cut shoe's nose and Winter was no longer of an issue. These were cold-weather sandals, which after a short walk matched boy's feet temperature with that of their exterior.

But exploding stones was so exciting that he did not notice and neither cared for his ice-cold, soaked in grey slush extremities.

He also knew – when he made it to the class – that if he put sandals and socks under a red hot radiator they will be bone dry by the time the school is over. Running barefoot was fun and original. At home, the drying process was repeated placing wet again garment beside the huge coal-burning cast iron furnace, converted by the boy into a spaceship or a submarine when the heating season was over.

The coal and some threadbare tires were burning. Not much of the plastic which was rare and considered to be an imperialist's product. So there was no reason for blown out of proportion air pollution warnings. For as long as sandals and socks dried out nicely.

The front yard had a lovely orchard made up of
the Japanese cherry trees producing sour,
dark fruit.
The boy harvested them into the plastic yellow
bucket when the time came for Grandma to
make delicious confitures and liquers.
In the winter, privy of produce and foliage the
orchard resembled platoons of scarecrows.
Naked thin branches sprouting even thinner,
nasty black fingers waving in unison along
with the biting wind were quite chill to watch.
Mama occupied one larger room in the attic.
To the boy the entry was strictly forbidden.
But he was Brave! He was the Stone Wrecker!
He was the Teeth Shaker!
He had winter sandals. made just for him.
He was curious, scared out of his wits, but
sneaked into Mama's sanctuary when she was
away searching for another unfamiliar man to
replace the current one.

Finding plenty she proudly admitted later.
Some, while not drunk were nice to the Boy.
He can recall stories they told him to this day.
Math lessons no.
Nothing wrong with that. He was wearing
an idiot's label in school.
Entering Mama's premises was like going on
the journey to fantastic worlds, where everything,
to the specks of dust and cobweb filigrees, had its
place. Shelved books pages were numbered.
Even for the ones written in a language
he did not understand.
Bed covers were folded so intricately...
Once touched it was impossible to put them back
into the same form.
A world of perfection contrasted hugely with
constant disorder downstairs, where the Boy
and Grandma lived.

Beside the bed was a small table.
A book with a sticking out page marker on it.
And on the book's front cover rested
a red pack of cigarettes.
It said Pall Mall in white.
The Boy - ten or eleven by then was
mesmerized. The pack lured him into a taboo.
Everything else became unimportant.
Swiftly, like Rikki-Tikki-Tawi – his hero from
the beloved Jungle – the Boy as quietly as he
could fought floor squeaks and the distance
to the pack.
This done, he sank his fingers into the
red box and pulled out one long, white cylinder
filled with light brown, slightly moist and
deliciously fragrant substance.
Next, he ruffled the package in an attempt to
make it look like nothing was amiss.
And it appeared to be O.K.

Savouring the tobacco aroma of the nonfiltered
Pall-Mall as noiselessly as he could, he
made his way back to the door and: "What are
you doing up there?" he heard from downstairs.
Grandma just came back from the garden
unexpectedly. "She comes back and finds out
you went to her room she'll go nuts," said
Grandma. She knew her daughter well.
But Mama didn't come back for several days.
Smoked through fits of heavy cough by the
Boy and his friend Chris the cigarette
Was gone, followed by Chris,
who died in the future at the age of 67.
The Boy smokes still.
Plain cigarettes always.
Every one a tribute to the stolen first.
And to Chris.
Mama came back all alone and in a foul mood.
Without a word, she disappeared upstairs
closing the door with a bang.

In the morning, after breakfast, which like every other day was made of two big softboiled eggs, before the boy went to school,
Grandma asked him to fill up the plastic yellow bucket with water from the green hand pump in the kitchen almost to the brim - the house had no other water sources back then.
She told him then to cut the thinnest and longest twigs from the nearby cherry tree, to wrap them into a nice bundle and to soak them - thin ends first - into the yellow bucket.
The Boy asked what's this for? "You'll see" answered Grandma. And off he went.
School...
The biology teacher, whom the Boy didn't mind was talking something about plants and fertilization.
The classroom had a big fish tank with fish in it.
Lazy, fat and very relaxed.

To the Boy's slightly agitated state of mind, who was trying to figure out why Grandma needed twigs, water and the yellow bucket the fish behaviour was unacceptable.
It just felt unjust.
He decided to disrupt that arrogant calmness...
His eyes made a full 360 scan of the classroom.
There it was!
A stuffed squirrel as old as the branch it was attached to with the tail like a brown leafless twig, its blind glass eyes focused on something beyond the classroom walls.
While the teacher chalked some confusions on the blackboard, her back facing the boredom of students, the Boy grabbed the opportunity.
With precise slowness he detached the fluffy cadaver from the branch and slid – precisely and slowly onto his chair. "Shit! I am good".

He sang victory inside his head, while dullness
covered his face.
Lights went off as some slides were to be
shown on the pull down screen.
Patterns - quite interesting and obtained from
the microscopically dead biology appeared,
strangely similar to the print on a cheap
window curtains in Grandma's
and his room downstairs.
In the class: some boys started to scratch and
adjust their genitals, others tried to ease-up
their hard-ons. Some others went on touching
girls' budding tits which, in some cases was
welcome and in some other was not.
While the psychedelic stroboscope, controlled
by the teacher run incessantly on the screen, the
Boy put the squirrels' tail between his teeth and
crawled towards the fish tank.

In its shadows he slowly rose, took the dead tail out of his mouth and, reaching the tank's brim with his left hand, he gently eased his trophy down into the water with his right.

Some shimmering bubbles popped out in the wake of the drowning rodent and that was it.

When the show came to an end and the lights went on again, the Boy was at his desk projecting calm innocence.

The bell rang. The class was over.

The teacher screamed.

The pupils flocked at the door, anxious to burst into the Lysol scented corridors froze.

The teacher screamed again, pointing towards the fish tank.

And again, this time directly at the Boy.

"Youuu!", she almost choked. "You!". "You did this!", and she was at the tank, pulling wet rodent out of the water, along with a fish caught in its fur.

Yes, I did", the Boy calmly admitted.
Her jaw down just for a spell,
the teacher was speechless.
Then, shaking the dripping taxidermy in front
of his face she's got her voice back and half
yelled, half hissed "I'll take revenge!".
"Revenge is the domain of ignoble", the Boy
said, recalling a quote from a book he recently
finished reading. Islands of Madness it was
called. Although he didn't understand all of it,
that particular phrase stuck, kicked him out of
class and prompted a disciplinary hearing in
principal's office. The Boy was considered a
lost cause at school, so the principal said "Just
don't do it again". And that was it.
On the way home the Boy was analyzing
his behaviour. Found nothing wrong with it.
Also he decided that a wet dead rodent looked
much better when wet than dry and dusty,
wired to that branch above aquarium

House was cold. So was the water in the yellow
bucket along withe bundle of twigs he made
in the morning.
"Go get some coal and kindling wood" his
Grandma commanded with unreadable
expression on her face. This, upon Boy's
experience did not promise anything good.
He started the fire, waited a bit before adding
coal chunks on top of the burning wood at the
right time and he knew when.
Because after doing this for many years he turned
to be an expert.
Squatting in front of the stove he listened to the
red hot music coming from its cast iron gut,
warming the yellow bucket,
the room and himself.
He didn't know if Mama was home.
A long time ago he decided that it was
none of his business.

Grandma gave him something to eat at the old round table for six. But it could be extended to sit twelve. He started to eat, using the fork and the knife properly the way Grandma taught him.

The door in Mama's room opened and then she was downstairs instantly. "Like riding a broom", he concluded.

"He doesn't know table manners!" Mama yelled through white toothpaste foam and the toothbrush she held in her mouth. "You rise him like a peasant!", she continued accusingly. The Boy knew she wants to just piss Grandma off, who patiently and successfully drilled the etiquette into him.

Grandma kept quiet. "Not just a peasant but also a thief!", Mama added.

"Ah", Grandma exhaled.

She's got an idea where this accusation was coming from.

The Boy was reading a book, completely detached from the two women exchange.
The massive stove radiated a massive waves of heat and except for the both Mama and Grandma raised voices the house was quiet.
"Go and wash", urged Grandma. He went to the bathroom, took a leak, flushing the toilet with water from the hand pump in the kitchen poured into the quart made of aluminum which had the swastika stamped on its side.
The quart was extremely handy but in the future it got lost.
Stark naked he walked into the room.
He felt some commotion behind his back, a little slurping noise and a scorching pain on his buttocks.
Then at the rear side of his thighs, on his lower back and a few licks on his ribs, as he was dancing a mad dance trying to escape the flogging.

Beat him! Beat him! The little thief peasant shit!" cheering Mama screeched. Grandma kept going, the Boy kept dancing and his brown skin was rapidly covered by a red swollen lattice.

'He's not just a thief who stole my smoke! This little bastard ruined my boobs! The most beautiful boobs on the Boardwalk! Beat him, beat him".

Mama laughed with a sadistic satisfaction standing in the doorway like a live menacing barricade making the escape impossible.

White toothpaste, now dry, was flaking away from the corners of her mouth and from the toothbrush handle she was still chewing on.

Grandma face, like his buttock was turning red and the hits became weaker and suddenly all stopped.

Grandma eyes were full of tears, of sadness and looking at the Boy with a plea for forgiveness

She dropped twigs into the yellow bucket and said "Your boobs eh? You little bitch"
"Did you think you could fuck a hockey team without consequences, eh?".
The Boy did not get what was this all about. "Bitch?". "Why bitch?". "She's not a dog", he mused while his butt screamed, so he didn't have to.
"Make your bed", said Grandma "and sleep on your stomach", she ordered, smearing some lard on his rear end.
He winced, gritted his teeth and kept silent. Tears were rolling down his cheeks, but no one noticed. Mama was upstairs already and Grandma was shortsighted anyway.
He couldn't sleep for awhile. Semi-awake he travelled the unknown universes, fought vicious armies of boobs, emerging a victor to the Grandma's wake -up call in the morning, next day.

For breakfast s he's got him the usual. Two soft boiled eggs, straight from the hen pen and a buttered slice of bread. They did not talk. She felt guilty and ashamed. He knew why and she was forgiven.
She was his feeding hand. He wasn't a dog. He did not bite. He dressed, took a leak behind the house, - so there was no need to pump flush water - grabbed his cardboard backpack, kissed Grandma in the cheek and left for school.
The backpack was cheap but heavy – used as a weapon often, when some bullies tried to beat the shit out of him – and run away when he didn't budge and started to swing the pack like bolas, this formidable South American weapon he's read about somewhere.
The backpack was touching his back and it hurt. Brave as he was, he endured.
He made to school in time.
Alone he sat at his desk.
The math teacher came.

The class was quiet.
Boy's butt was not.
He needed to squirm and rock on his
Squeaky chair.
The math teacher was an arsehole. He was also
a sadist. Because whenever he was beating
kid's open palm with a wooden ruler his
breathing was fast, his face was red and there
was a noticeable bulge growing in front of his
pants. And no matter how desperately the
teacher tried to be respected by his pupils, that
was something to talk and laugh about, making
children fearless, wanting to provoke him,
receiving punishment regardless.
The Boy kept squirming and moving in a vain
attempt to find part of his buttocks free
from swelling.
He couldn't.
The teacher came along and pulled his ear.
Hard.

He said "Stop moving".
The Boy couldn't. So his ear was pulled again.
Teacher's crotch started to expand.
The class noticed. The teacher pulled hair at the back of Boy's head. Hard. And harder.
And the crotch expanded more.
The class watched.
The teacher went for ear again swinging the wooden ruler in front of Boy's eyes.
And the Boy squirmed again. The pain in his lower end was excruciating.
He did not react to the teacher's actions as expected. He did not beg to stop, he did not plead for mercy.
Finding his efforts futile and the bulge withering the teacher said "Get out. You are banned from my math class for the rest of the school year". And with a cold satisfaction he added "You won't make to another grade.

You'll be digging trenches with the shovel for the rest of your life. That's what your kind is made for".

The future with the shovel and a trench was predicted for him too often.

He wasn't afraid of hard work so he couldn't care less. He was also a Space traveller.

For this one have to be brave. Always carry the cheap cardboard backpack.

Never leave home without it.

He did not wait for the next class where he would need to sit again.

He went home taking a longer route through the forest, where he was alone and could watch young pine trees. Their tops moving in the wind, navigating blue sky like the masts of his armada.

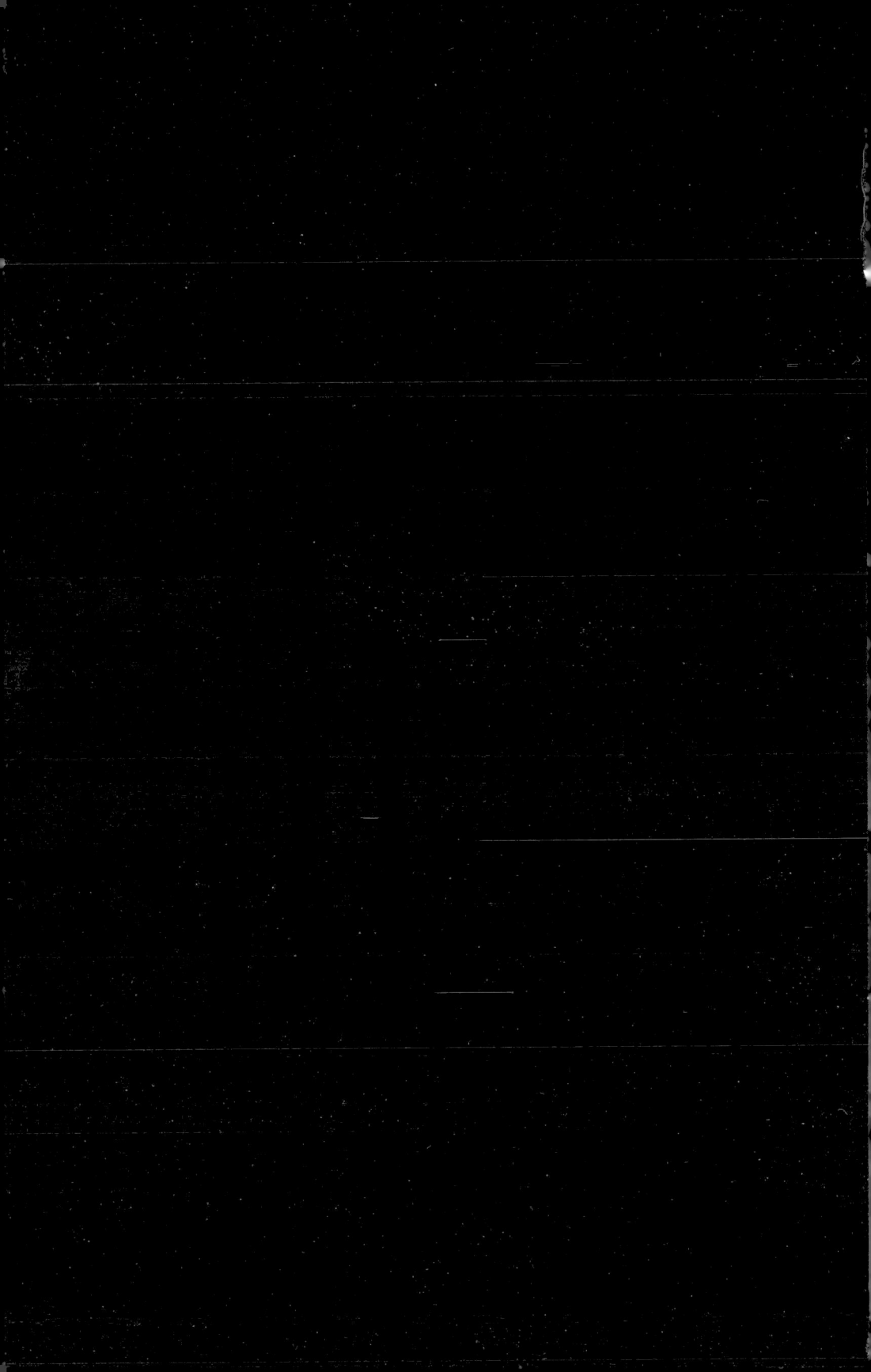